The True Story of SUPERMAN

By Louise Simonson

Illustrations by Mike Parobeck, Rick Burchett, and Don Desclos

A GOLDEN BOOK • NEW YORK

Western Publishing Company, Inc., Racine, Wisconsin 53404

On a distant dying planet called Krypton, a young couple put their only child into a tiny spaceship. The ship was too small to hold the couple, but their son fit snugly inside. Sadly they watched as the ship lifted into the sky.

A moment later the planet Krypton exploded. But the spaceship and the child inside were safe—speeding toward Earth.

The spaceship crashed into a field in Kansas on the farm of Jonathan and Martha Kent. The Kents took the baby home and named him Clark.

Clark was not an ordinary child. He could run faster than his friends and hear sounds from miles away. Nothing hurt him. He could even see through walls. His strange powers scared him.

One day the strangest thing of all happened. Clark jumped over the farmyard gate to do his after-school chores. Suddenly he was soaring in the air. "Ma! Pa!" he cried. "Look! I'm flying."

Later he asked his parents, "Why can I do these amazing things?"

So Jonathan Kent showed Clark the long-hidden spaceship from Krypton. "We don't know where you came from," Mr. Kent told his son. "But you have great powers and must always use them wisely."

Secretly Clark began to use his special powers to help people. One day he was visiting the city of Metropolis. Suddenly a plane began spinning out of control. Clark quickly flew into the sky and caught the plane just in time.

Lois Lane, ace reporter for the *Daily Planet* newspaper, was on the plane that Clark had saved. "He must be some kind of super man," she thought. And in the news story Lois later wrote, she called him Superman.

Clark returned home to his parents' farm. He was worried. If people knew about his double identity, how could he do good and still lead a normal life?

His parents had the perfect solution. Clark's mother made him a special costume to wear. Then no one would recognize him when he used his superpowers.

Clark was thrilled. Now he looked like what Lois Lane had called him. He looked like Superman!

Wearing his brand-new costume, Clark flew back to Metropolis. He soon got a job at the *Daily Planet*. Working as a reporter, he could learn about people's troubles. For many weeks he helped people as Clark Kent—and as Superman.

One afternoon Clark heard a distant cry for help and the *tick-tick-tick* of a bomb. He ducked out of sight and changed into his Superman costume. Then off he flew from the *Daily Planet* building.

Using his X-ray vision, Superman looked through the walls of a nearby building. He saw a janitor tied up in a dark basement—and two masked men with a bomb.

Superman sped into the basement.

"You saved me!" the janitor cried as Superman untied him.
Then Superman grabbed the bomb and flew high above the
building.

Boom! The bomb exploded a mile over Metropolis. But Superman wasn't hurt. His superstrong body blocked the explosion and protected the people and buildings below.

The next day Superman heard cries from a sinking ocean liner far out at sea. Faster than a speeding bullet, Superman flew to the ship. He lifted the heavy anchor and towed the ship to shore. The sailors and passengers shouted, "Hooray for Superman!"

The ship was safely docked when Superman smelled smoke. Miles away he saw people leaning out the windows of a burning building. In an instant he was there. Superman rescued the people and used his powerful lungs to help the firefighters put out the fire.

Superman heard another call for help. A bus had stalled on a railroad track, and a runaway train was about to crash into it!

In the nick of time, Superman pushed the bus to safety and stopped the out-of-control train.

Earth's greatest super hero had saved the day once again!

SPOTLIGHT ON

SUPERMAN

SECRET IDENTITY: Clark Kent

ALIAS: Man of Steel

OCCUPATION: Reporter for the *Daily Planet* newspaper

KNOWN RELATIVES: Jonathan and Martha Kent (parents on Earth), Jor-El and Lara (parents on Krypton, deceased)

BASE OF OPERATIONS: Metropolis, U.S.A.

HEIGHT: 6 feet 3 inches

WEIGHT: 225 pounds

EYES: Blue

HAIR: Black

POWERS: Superman has tremendous strength, a nearly indestructible body, and the ability to fly. His senses are supersharp: he can move and think faster than any other living thing on Earth, hear sounds that humans cannot hear, and see things from very far away—and through walls. Only kryptonite, a mineral from his home planet Krypton, can make his superpowers fail.